When We Grow Up
by
Kim Beatrice

DEDICATION

I dedicate this book to
Ingy and Dante
and
all the kids around
the world.

… Kim Beatrice

Hello, my name is Thomas.
When I grow up I would like
to drive a snow plough and
clear snow and ice from homes
and workplaces.

Hello, we are sally, Josh, Spotty and Tiger. When Sally and I grow up we would like to be artists and paint three headed green dragons.

Hello, we are Jill, Cameron and Sophia. When we grow up we would like to be librarians and read lots of books and learn about the world.

Hello, we are Dillon, Jemma, Collin and Miss Tracey who is holding the Lollipop stop sign. When we grow up we would like to be like Miss Tracey and keep all children safe when walking across the crossing.

Hello, my name is Peter and when I grow up I would like to be a Postman and deliver nice and important letters and parcels to your letterbox.

Hello, my name is Ben and when I grow up I would like to be a train driver and show passengers spectacular views on my journeys.

Hello, my name is Timothy and when I grow up I would like to be a diver and study dolphins and whales.

Hello, we are Zoe and Zac and
when we grow up we would
like to be scientists so we can
do experiments and make the
world a better place.

Hello, we are Lulu and Liam. When we grow up we would like to be professional dancers and entertain everyone.

Hello, my name is Olivia. When I grow up I would like to be a fire fighter to save people's lives and put out all the flames.

Hello, we are the 'Good Guys'. When we grow up we would like to be doctors and nurses to help you as soon as you need us.

Hello, my name is Max. When I grow up I would like to be a farmer and grow lots of fruit and vegetables to help feed people.

Hello, my name is Stacey. When I grow up I would like to be a baker and bake lots of breads and pastries.

Hello, my name is Pip. When I grow up I would like to be an author and write lots of funny stories.

Hello, we are Manu, Lisa and Christina. When we grow up we would like to remain close friends so if something goes wrong, one of us will always be there to help.

Hello, we are kids that love animals. When we grow up we would like to be zoo keepers so we can feed them and take care of them.

Hello, we are Jarrod, Kate and Pete. When we grow up we would like to be musicians and play really cool music for everyone.

Hello, we are Keith and Kelly. When we grow up we would like to be sailors on a navy ship so we can protect our land from nasty enemies.

Hello, we are Roger, Annie and Benjamin. When we grow up we would like to be volunteers to pack food boxes for the needy in our country.

Hello, we are Rick and Rachel. When we grow up we would like to be professional softball players and travel the world to compete with other players.

Hello, we are Trinny and Timothy. When I grow up I would like to be a hairdresser just like Trinny and give really cool haircuts.

Hello, my name is Kelvin.
When I grow up I would like
to own a pet shop so I can care
for them and get them ready
for their new owner.

Hello, my name is Shane.
When I grow up I would like
to be a 'Jack of all Trades' to do
any job that is needed.

Hello, my name is Anthony.
When I grow up I would like
to be a chef and make yummy
meals for everyone.

Hello, my name is Lisa. When I grow up I would like to be a school teacher and teach all my students everything they need to know.

Hello, my name is Alison.
When I grow up I would like
to be a photographer and take
lots of photos of weddings.

Hello, my name is Katy. When I grow up I would like to be a swimming instructor so I can teach everyone how to swim so they won't drown.

Hello, my name is Lucas.
When I grow up I would like
to be a driving instructor and
teach you safely how to drive.

… all we have to do now is grow!

The End